JOURNEY TO CHINA

JOURNEY TO CHINA

❖

LOUANE K. BEYER

Library of Congress Control Number: 2014902815
ISBN: Hardcover   978-1-4931-7409-6
                 Softcover   978-1-4931-7410-2
                 eBook   978-1-4931-7408-9

Printed in the United States of America by BookMasters, Inc
Ashland OH
May 2014

Rev. date: 04/26/2014

To order additional copies of this book, contact:
Xlibris LLC
1-888-795-4274
www.Xlibris.com
Orders@Xlibris.com
551875

CONTENTS

ILLUSTRATIONS

1. Cover: Scenery As Viewed From Airplane As It Approaches Beijing
2. Asian Princess
3. Chinese Pagoda
4. Panda Bear
5. Bees
6. Two American Girls and Chinese Pen Pal With Her Grandfather
7. Dragon Boats - Ancient
8. Airplane Leaving China Airport
9. Ring Of Fire
10. The Land Of The Dragon

Xlibris Illustrator: Kenny Estrella

   Louane Beyer
   Roger Beyer and our grandchildren
   Emilee Lindseth
   Adam Beyer
   Abigail Beyer
   Allie Beyer
   Nathan Beyer

ACKNOWLEDGMENT

This is our third book in this series that was written with input and advice from my husband, Roger, along with each of our grandchildren who in some way provided assistance in the narrative or sketched for the illustrations. It was a journey for me as I learned so much in watching videos, reading material, and using pure imagination. In addition as I read about the Grand Canal and the Dragon Boat Races, I was so excited to include Bemidji, Minnesota into the story as each year, a Dragon Boat Festival is held on Lake Bemidji. There is a real connection to China and this festival right in the area where I live. Thank you to the many people who have purchased my two other books, Six Days Inside A Mountain and Lost In The Amazon. The current book, Journey to China, is a sequel to the last two books. This is another heart warming story for the whole family. It is a gem for sure.

DEDICATION

This dedication goes to the global bee keepers that strive to keep the bee colonies producing. The importance of this is that more than 90 crops in the United States alone depend on the honey bee for pollinating the crops.

Bees have been making honey for thousands of years. An active colony can visit more than a million flowers and produce over 2 pounds of honey in a single day. The color and taste of honey depends on the type of flower nectar. Our family has been active in maintaining a hive each season for many years. We can distinguish the difference in the honey from the apple tree flowers in the spring and the clover in the summer.

In recent years across our country alone about one third of the bee colonies have been dying off. The worker bees leave the hive and do not return. The disappearance of the worker bee causes colony collapse disorder. Some factors that could be the cause are pests, parasites, poor nutrition, diseases, pesticides, and fewer foraging places. Some of these factors point to disorientation and poor nutrition after being exposed to pesticides. The worker bee flies out of the hive to

collect pollen and nectar then doesn't have the strength
to bring it back. This causes a big problem.

There is consensus that co-operative agencies, bee
keepers and agricultural producers can find solutions to
improve honey bee health.

CHAPTER 1

Letter from Chinese pen pal arrives

A summer storm was passing through the valley with echoes of loud thunder rolling and booming. It was Saturday morning with Allie and Abby sitting on the window seat sketching on their I-pads. Allie was checking on the photos she had submitted to YouTube and Abby a cartoon she had drafted. Suddenly there was a clap of thunder so close it shook the window panes. The power flickered off and on. Both the girls jumped away from the window screaming in fright. They were alarmed by the strong wind they could hear as the rain poured down.

Abby's mom, Susan, suggested that they could go to their room where it would be quieter and assured them that the storm would soon pass. Abby's brother, Nate, who was propped up on pillows on the living room floor watching a cartoon on the television was happy that the power stayed on.

Soon the rest of the family gathered in the living room to watch the dark clouds fearful that a tornado could be looming within the formation.

Just then, their dad, Brad, pulled into the garage running into the house exclaiming, "Wow! What a downpour. We really need this rain as it is so dry. I sent the construction crew home for the day as it will be too wet in the work area. The building we are constructing is nearly completed and I was relieved that the rain held off long enough to allow the crew to close the openings."

He went to the washroom to towel off his wet hair and on to the kitchen for a cup of hot coffee. Returning he reached down and ruffled Nate's hair as Nate looked up and smiled. Brothers, Peter and Adam, stood around for a while and decided to head off to the kitchen for some breakfast as they were hungry.

Brad looked around at his family with a lump in his throat about how happy he was now that he felt strong and well enough to return to work.

He recalled a month of rehabilitation to restore his stability after the concussion he had received as a result of the airplane crash in the Amazon Rain Forest of Peru. He learned to appreciate the support from his family and friends while his strength returned. The dizziness was gone for good he hoped. He stood looking out of the big window with a secure feeling in the two story house that he had built several years ago. The summer storm with the rain shafts pouring down was moving away. He felt small hands reach up into his hands. By his side were Abby, his daughter, and his niece, Allie. The smiles they gave him reached right into his heart. They were both such beautiful girls. Allie with her shoulder length brown hair accenting her oval shaped face was growing this summer. On the other side of him stood his daughter, Abby, whose face was more heart shaped with hair that had a reddish streak running on one side. As cousins, they seemed more like twins as they were born only days apart. Often times, their personalities matched so close to one another.

Just then the doorbell rang and the girls ran to see who could be coming to visit in this weather. It was the mailman with a special delivery. To their surprise, it was for them! He had them sign for it and commented that it was from China. His rain cloak was dripping rain as he smilingly said, "This weather is for ducks. Lucky for you that I got an early start or I might not have made it over the bridge. It may have water running over it now and I will be going back the other route. Enjoy the letter from China."

Allie looked at the address to see if it was from her mom and dad, who were in Beijing, shaking her head in disappointment. Abby put her hand on Allie's shoulder saying, "Allie, I know you would have liked to hear from your mom and dad but for second best this is from Sadako, our pen pal. Let's take it to our room and see what she is sending us special delivery." Allie with a soft sob accepted a hug from her cousin and agreed that it would be fun to open the package. She went on to say, "Maybe my mom and dad will call me soon on Skype. They've been gone now for 3 months and I miss them very much. I am happy and so grateful to be here with your family who accepts me as one of the family. It is just not the same as if I was at home with mom and dad."

They turned as they heard a small voice ask, "What is Skype? Is that an app that I could use on my I-pad?" It was Nate with Abby responding that he should go ask mom as she could describe it better. She did add that it was how Allie speaks to her mom and dad. Nate ran off calling for mom who came down the hall and asked him to come to the kitchen for his breakfast. He then asked her what Skype is? Mom replied, "It is an Internet feature that is called video chat. Dad and your uncle hook up on the computer and we talk with Allie's parents. Remember several weeks ago when they called and we saw them on the television screen.

Wasn't that neat?" Then Nate remembered and commented that perhaps soon they would call again.

Down the hall, the girls opened the envelope that was sort of damp from the rain. Thank goodness that the contents were protected. Inside was a picture that Sadako had drawn. The girls gasped when they saw it was the likeness of the 'Asian Princess with Songbird' figurine. The colors were incredibly vivid and clear with reds, black, blue, and the white face. They couldn't read what she wrote as it was in Chinese. Their teacher at school knew a Chinese exchange student who would interpret for them. Allie looked up the drawing on her I-pad and read that it was a prized Chinese art created a millennium ago. She said, "If only we could speak to Sadako via our I-pads. We could send her designs we've been working on. The Chinese government censors the use of the internet.

Asian Princess With Songbird

They do not have the freedom that we have. I wonder when or even if I will be going to China and if my parents contact me to come, would it be possible to meet Sadako?" Abby agreed that it would be so cool.

Then added "I can hardly wait until we can have our teacher, Mrs Ames, translate her letter to see what she has written us. Now that school is out for the summer, it may take longer to get in touch with her. Let's go call and ask her."

To their disappointment when they called their teacher, the message machine was activated so they left a message. It took two days until she called the girls back. She was almost as excited as the girls about the sketch and the letter from Sadako and told them to come to the school that afternoon as she knew the Chinese exchange student was available.

Abby's mom, Susan, accompanied the girls to the school library as she was interested in the project as well. The teacher, the girls, and Susan had a few minutes to visit. The teacher remarked that it was a co-incidence that the girls chose a Chinese pen pal and now Allie's parents were in China. Abby's mom explained, "In the United States, the bee population loss is alarming." She relayed that she had read the other day that more than one third of the bee colonies perished over the winter that will have a huge economic impact to the food industry. The reasons are complex. According to the girls' grandfather who monitors this tells us that one in three bites of food is reliant on the honey bee for production. In addition he said that 80 % of cherry trees and all of the almond trees depend on the honey bee for pollination. It works like this he says that most all flowers produce a sweet liquid that honey bees are attracted to and they make honey from the nectar. The honey bee workers collect pollen that is most important to us. As they travel from flower to flower, the pollen brushes off onto a special pollen receiving stigma in the center. In a nutshell this is called 'pollination' and allows all flowering plants to reproduce. Thereby the honey bee is necessary in the pollination of crops.

Actually it has become a global issue. There are no real answers to what is killing off the bees. Some studies show it is mites and others say pesticides, chemicals or toxic substances. Allie's dad, Sam, has been interested in bees ever since at about the age of 10 when he and his dad set up a hive in their back yard as a 4-H project. Many people in the neighborhood were so delighted as they saw how the bees not only improved the apple crop and the gardens but also thrived in the honeysuckle hedge. He went to get his doctorate in education but never forgot the bees and has kept abreast with the latest issues. The country of China has taken to manually pollinate plants, crops, and trees as the bees are de-populating there also. This interested him that led him to do research on it. He contacted the US Ag Dept that gave him a grant to travel to China to attend the Peking University that has become a center for teaching and research. The University has combined the research on fundamental scientific issues and because this is of grave concern, many international entities are attending. It is hopeful that some real solutions could be reached. Allie's mom, Kate, will be studying religion at the university as well. Allie stayed with us to complete the school year. We hope that soon she will join her parents. "Isn't this just fascinating that they were able to take off a year from their jobs to do this?" she said.

The exchange student had joined them listening to what was going on and agreed. She explained that she did not have much time between classes at summer school and would it be agreeable to take Sadako's letter with her to translate it for the girls this week. It was more than a bit disappointing but they agreed. She said she would write it out in English then return it to the teacher.

To keep the two girls occupied while waiting for the translation, Abby's mom suggested that the girls search magazines, newspapers, books, and their I-pads for articles/photos/stories that portray life here in the United States then assemble them into a scrap book to send to Sadako. Because this is learning about each other's culture, this would be an excellent method to show and tell Sadako about how we live along with what our interests are. She suggested for them to look for weather, sports, fashion, comics, malls, advertising, toys, and even to include some recipes that our family likes. Then when the exchange student has written out what Sadako said in her letter, you could sort of be ready to share your activities. The idea sparked great interest as they ran down the hall to their room.

CHAPTER 2

Flight Plans made to go to China

It took several days until their teacher called to say that the letter from Sadako was translated. To the girls' surprise, she added that the exchange student would meet with them to answer any questions they had. Abby's mom was free this morning so off they went to the library.

Abby and Allie were so excited to hear what the letter said with the exchange student reading it to them with the beginning of an introduction that her name is Mia Sadako. I am so happy that you two chose me for a pen pal and that our teachers agreed to this project. While I am an only child in my family, I have several cousins who live close by so we ride our bikes to the school with classes six days a week for 10 months out of the year.

I really like school with math, science, geography, and especially music as I love to sing. Our music teacher told us that many of our melodies make use of an octave of five notes do, re, mi, so, and la. She has studied music from around the world and taught us that our melodic structure is different as it tends to flow on without repetition. She brought some records to compare how western tunes tend to build by repetition. I like to hum tunes even while I do chores at home.

We have computers in our classroom to use for research but our access is limited. She went on to say that she was happy to hear that Allie liked school, sports, unique friends, and the description of the school project about one state in the country. Allie had a map of her chosen state drawings of the state tree, bird, flower, and flag along with some statistics of who the governor is, what are special features, and how many people live there. At our school, we do not have grades but levels of achievement. Then to Abby, I was happy to hear that you also like to sing and hum tunes. You are both so lucky to each have an I-pad to do drawings and play games on them. Abby, I was interested in the 'Inside Government Project' that you did for Girl Scouts. I could not believe that Mayor Ness allowed you to sit in his chair. You probably learned much about local offices with the questions your group asked. In my province, it is too far away for us to travel to so I am learning from you.

We have a small house yellow in color. I live with my parents and grandparents. This arrangement helps to share the work in our vegetable garden where the main plant is Zhongmu garlic, a specialty of our region. We live in the outskirts of Zhengzhou that lies on the south bank of the Yellow River. The city is large with more than eight million people in the area but where we have our house and garden, it is quiet. My grandfather and father often go to the river to catch carp fish for a variety in our meals. Mostly we eat chicken that is steamed or boiled with rice and vegetables. My grandmother used to do most of the cooking but she is getting frail so now my mother does that. She likes to add special sauces and flavorings that my grandparents like as they are unable to digest lactose which is milk sugar. Some days, my mother lets me help prepare the meals. We grow vegetables in our garden that we sell at a stand close to our home.

We are a quiet family except for my grandfather who loves to chuckle and tell us all sorts of stories about what happened when he was growing up. I will be anxious to get another letter from you both.

As the letter ended there, the exchange student explained that she was from Beijing and was thrilled to have been chosen to travel to America to live with a family for a year on a student visa. My name is Soo Ling. I haven't been to the region that Sadako resides in as in China the average people don't travel like the people in America. I know there is a sizable poultry plant in that province and that it employs many people.

I am learning more about your country and I will study hard. My English is improving each day. She said, "Since your teacher, Mrs Ames, told me that Allies's parents are in China, I wonder if I could give you some information about China. First of all, China is called 'The Land of The Dragon.' I have studied the history of Imperial China way back to AD 960 with the Song Dynasty at which time the country was well over

1000 years old. Just imagine how new your country is in comparison but both countries have had many wars. Back to China though, Manchuria that is located to the north of China was a powerful rival. Zhao, the leader of China, struggled for his beloved country even though there were many hardships for the peasants." She went on to tell that he tried to use the teachings of Confucius. Actually what was happening there could be the same situation as in the United States in the past months. There had been many cutbacks and budget restrictions to lower the debt on all levels in the government and with the states raising taxes which separates the poor and the rich even more. Some states were raising taxes on the rich to help the poor.

In our country at that time, he tried to ask the people to live within their means but the rich land owners rebelled. The Mongols invaded China in the 1200s led by Genghis Khan who over took the Yuan dynasty. Great floods and rebellions drove out the invaders. She added, "I am so proud of the rich heritage, the centuries of evolution, and the inventions of my country. Our new president, Xi Jinping, is recognizing the value to replace government led investments with market forces involving innovation and sound development. Just call on me if you need any more assistance". She bowed and thanked them. It amazed both Allie and Abby as they watched with awe and admiration. They in turn thanked their teacher for this project.

Upon their return to the house, Nate greeted them with excitement saying, "While you were at the library,

Allie's parents called to tell us that they are going to contact us on Skype at 7:00 tonight. They have some news to share with all of us including Grandpa and Grandma. I wonder what they want to tell us." His mom gave him a big hug thanking him for taking the message saying, "I suppose I should call Grandpa and Grandma to invite them to dinner." Nate said, "Mom, they already know and Grandma is bringing a pot roast and apple pie. She told me to be sure to tell you as she knows you have a lot to do. I don't like pot roast so could we have mac/cheese or pizza. Dad knows too and is coming home early.

Peter and Adam are out in the back yard so they know." His mom shook her head in amazement.

At 7:00 p.m., the equipment beeped and there they were both of Allie's parents. Brad greeted his brother, "Sam, you are prompt for sure.

Hi to Kate also from all of us." Sam also greeted the family and especially his daughter, Allie. He went on to say, "Time is limited. The research director of the department received special approval as this call involves the family so I want to get to the highest priority items discussed first. Dad, good to see you. Will you do me a favor regarding the bee project. We are doing research that besides scent and color that flowers have to attract the bees, there may be a third factor that is electrical attraction which is something our family never considered when we had hives. I will write you a letter regarding the research that has been done that states that more than 90% of bees are positively charged and flowers are negatively charged. The study is interesting and enlightening in pollination. Would you check with the county agent to check if there are neonicotinoid insecticides used on seeds planted in our part of the country as some international countries have banned some of the neonicotinoid insecticides due to the high acute risk to bees during spring planting? There is information available that the insecticides cause disorientation in the bees which in turn don't eat properly and weaken them. I will include that in my letter. Now on to the happier item, Brad. You set an example for us when you, Peter, and Adam traveled to South America on business. Because you are feeling back to your old self, Kate and I have discussed that you and the family travel to China to accompany our daughter, Allie. I would not feel safe any other way. My grant will pro-rate the trip as it is a family member. Yeah, I know another house and pet for Mom and Dad to take care of. I wanted to tell you out right so you can confer among yourselves if this is possible. We can accomodate some of you to stay on campus with us and I would make all the arrangements should you agree. The university is the largest institution of higher learning in this country. They have made an effort to combine the research on scientific issues with the training of staff. It is remarkable how busy it is here but, in the end, we are looking forward to have Allie here so she can learn about the wonders of this country as well. I am sorry to have taken almost all of our allotted time speaking and not listening. We can call you soon but thought it best to have you all here to listen to our current proposition. We could celebrate the birthdays of Abby and Allie while you are here. I hope that Peter, Adam, and Nate are catching some fish in the creek—the screen went blank as the connection was broken. Grandma and Grandpa said, "We didn't even get to say farewell." Everyone was quiet and thoughtful as they looked at the blank screen.

Brad was the first to speak up with a question, "Well, what do you think of us going to China? First of all, we need to see if Grandpa and Grandma would help with Buddy. We could get the neighbors to keep the yard up and watered. With these dry conditions and the persistent drought, you have enough with Sam's and your areas. With the rain we just got at least we don't have a fire danger anymore. There will be much to plan for as the trip would take us away at least 6 days." He turned to Allie only to see that Adam had already consoled her with a high five. Brad continued on saying, "Allie, I am sorry that you didn't get much chance to say anything but your dad and mom will call on the telephone soon. Come here, our dear little girl, and give uncle a big hug. This will be a huge adjustment for you to leave our country for about eight months and we will miss you terribly. You will be with your mom and dad though." He watched in amazement as no one was saying anything. It was as if they were spell bound. Then finally Nate said, "Now I know what Skype is." That was followed with laughter from the family.

Chapter 3

Arrive in Beijing

During the next two days, a flurry of telephone calls between China and the United States were made to make flight arrangements. The dads decided that the international flight would depart from San Francisco to Beijing. Brad double checked the visas for each of them to ensure that there would be no problems. Then he took up the task of checking on credit cards he could use in China and what currency would be required.

With these checks in place, he put an employee in charge of the work crew in the complex and houses he was building. It took all of two days for his part. The neighbors agreed to take care of the yard with the pets going to the grandparent's house. Susan took charge of clothing needs and items needed for about 6 days. Peter and Adam had experience of living out of a backpack and what would be needed. She knew Nate would be easy to accommodate but the girls were more selective. Allie needed the most space for clothes as she would be staying in China. The last detail was what they would take with them in the way of Ipads, Ipods, and Iphones through security.

At last, the family was packed and ready to drive to the local airport. As they drove out of the driveway, Brad and Susan were confident that the lists they had made were completed. It was all quiet. No one spoke. It was as if each of them was thinking of what was happening. Nate broke the silence saying, "We are really going to China. I hope we all come back. I miss home already. Grandpa and Grandma will be all alone. I am glad that they have Buddy to keep them company." He choked back tears.

For once no one teased him. His mom put her arm around him assuring him that all will be fine. We will have an exciting adventure ahead.

She was about to turn to the children when all of a sudden a big deer jumped out of the ditch nearly straight into the front fender. It required some deft reaction on the driver's part. Brad excitedly said, "Whew, thank goodness I was alert and none of you screamed." It seemed to bring the children to life as they babbled at the same time as they approached the local airport where they would catch the interconnecting flight to San Francisco.

After they had checked in their luggage it was a relief with Brad commenting to Susan, "It was a good idea that you decided to pre-mail most of Allie's items. It still seems like so much luggage and we were so careful to limit what we packed but look at all these bags. Oh well, lets get some refreshments as we have about an hour before take off.

I'd like a sundae." He looked around to get orders from the family. It did not take long before the announcement was heard that it was time to board.

Brad walked close to Peter and Adam inquiring how they were feeling but they shrugged their shoulders smiling. This reassured Brad that they had no qualms about flying. Brad and Susan took Nate to sit with them while the older children were seated in front of them. Allie and Abby were anxiously anticipating their first flight. The cabin attendant re-assured them that once airborne they would enjoy the two hour flight to San Francisco. It all went well once they were airborne. Nate who was seated with his parents changed places with his mom so he could look out the window. He turned to ask his mom and dad, "What are clouds made of?

They look so different up here than from the ground up. I remember Grandma used to sing a song while I was swinging. It went higher than than the clouds, higher than a jet plane and more. Now here I am up here higher than the clouds. The clouds look so puffy and white. I am going to look up clouds on my Ipad." They smiled at each other.

It didn't seem long before the announcement came to prepare for landing.

The children were amazed at the size of the airport and all the planes going and coming. Brad and Susan located the flight information board to verify the Air China schedule and seated the children close by. A young man seated close to them struck up a conversation first with the boys asking them questions about where they were going. He introduced himself as Yuan Kim. He acted amazed that the family was going to Beijing just like himself. The boys visited with him about where he lived and which flight he was scheduled to take. Peter offered that they were flying on Air China with the airplane a Boeing 777. His parents were close by double checking the gate which was scheduled to leave within the hour.

Yuan apologized and explained he was on a different airline to China.

Yuan mentioned to Adam," I see you have an Ipad and do you have the game 'Clash of the Clans' on it?" Adam shook his head that he did and played it often. Peter asked Yuan if he played video games he liked as 'Call of Duty?' Yuan's face lite up as he responded that was his favorite.

The noise from the incoming and departing jets was loud and often the conversation had to be checked until the noise abated.

Their mom came to check on the children which distracted them for a moment. Little did anyone know that Yuan inserted a digital tracking device disc into the seam of Peter's backpack and little did they even suspect that he was a member of the Chinese Government's Central Commission. The family gathered to walk toward their gate as they had already gone through security check. Only moments later the passenger announcement came that they were ready to receive passengers loading for the 11 hour flight.

Once airborne, the boys checked to make sure their Ipads were in airplane mode then looked up the Boeing Jet 777. Surprised they shared the information with their dad and Nate. The plane is the world's largest twin jet capacity to carry over 300 passengers with the first flight on June 12, 1977 at a possible top speed of 990 KPH and ceiling 37,900 feet. It was amazing information and they kept researching the information on Google.

Soon the children took naps until the meal was delivered. Later they watched some movies and settled in. Adam walked back to his parents seats and asked his mom if he could sit with them for awhile. He said, "I hear this buzzing in my head. It is like the sound of the worn out bulbs on a florescent light fixture. I asked Peter if he heard that sound as well and he did but just slightly. Mine is more intense and I would like to nap." His mom and dad exchanged glances as Adam was not one to complain of headaches and exchanged seats with him.

The time passed so quickly when the announcement to put the tray tables to an upright position and seat belts buckled signs were given. Allie was the most excited as she was to see her mom and dad. Adam awoke and felt refreshed so he went back to his assigned seat.

As the airplane circled for landing, Brad asked the children to look out of the window to get their first sight of Beijing. They could see that the city was located at the northern tip of what looked like a triangle opening to the south and east of Beijing. It was shielded to the north, northwest and west by mountains. There did look to be an agricultural heartland with encroaching desert steppes. Nate was the first to call out that he spied the 'Great Wall of China.' There it was in view across the northern part of the Beijing municipality. Brad added, "The Great Wall of China was built on the rugged landscape to defend the area against nomadic invasions from the steppes. We will take a tour of this great wonder."

With that, the airplane landed. There awaiting them were Sam and Kate to greet the family and hug their daughter, Allie. They were all happy to be able stretch their legs after the long hours on the airplane.

CHAPTER 4

The Great Wall of China

The two brothers, Sam and Brad, got the family situated then began the task of retrieving a mountain of luggage. While they were waiting, Sam said, "I have a car waiting to take us to the hotel. I made reservations to one close to the campus of the university. At first, I considered renting a cottage then changed my mind as the hotel has all the amenities which include a big pool and game room. We can set up a schedule for doing some tours after the family has settled in and the time change catches up with you. Kate and I want to spend the first night with Allie. We missed her. We have learned so much in the few months that we have been here. Beijing is a fascinating place. While you are here, we will see some of the places that Beijing is renown for such as its opulent palaces, temples, gardens, tombs, and gates. There are so many art treasures. You will not believe the university and I am humbled to have been offered the time to study here. How are you feeling? With all the plans we have had to discuss, I overlooked asking you."

As the suitcases came down the carousel, Brad nodded about the hotel and the reservations said,

"You know, Bro, I am really feeling good. It takes an experience that I had to be thankful for my family. It is still almost unimaginable what my boys did to save our lives in the remote area of the Amazon Rain Forest and it all seems like a dream. This trip is just what we needed to spend some time together and I am looking forward to some time alone with you. Do they have a ping pong table somewhere that we could take up a challenge against each other? It has been a long time since you and I have had the chance to play a few rounds."

Sam never got a chance to reply as he stared at the number of suitcases and wondered how they would fit in the small car he had ordered. He hailed a taxi to pull in next to the car parked on the curb to assist the families. They all laughed as the taxi driver mumbled something that they couldn't understand as he looked at how many suitcases there were. It was an undertaking that required the help of Brad, Sam, Peter, and Adam.

In the taxi, Peter asked his mom if she remembered the young Chinese guy that was visiting with them at San Francisco Airport? She said, "Yes, I recall he seemed so polite and friendly. Why do you ask?" Peter told her that he had seen Yuan at the Beijing Airport and he wouldn't even look their way. He added that Yuan had told him he was taking a different airline to China. It seems sort of strange. He shrugged it off as they wound their way to the hotel.

The whole family was amazed at the hotel that was chosen for them as it was like a sky scraper to the family from a small farming, desert community in southwestern America. The vehicles pulled into the front loading area and immediately there was a number of friendly staff to assist them with luggage and the checking in process. The children were silent and watched in awe. Finally Nate spoke. "This is like a movie.

Are you sure we can find our way in this tall building?" His uncle gave him a pat on the back in assurance that all was in order saying to him, "Nate, wait until you see the water park and exercise room that is here.

You will be thrilled as we know how much you like to swim."

With that Kate, Sam and Allie left to go to the university bidding them all a good night and an offering to set up some tours for tomorrow. Sam said to call him in the morning.

In the suite the family was too excited to do much but each described how they felt. They had already experienced so much. Adam spoke first saying, "We are in a foreign country. I wonder how different the places and people will be. When I studied geography, I never imagined that first dad, Peter and I would travel to South America. Now here we are in China. I feel excited about what we will see in the next few days." Of course, Abby was already lonesome without her cousin, Allie.

Susan looked at her family thinking what to do to adjust and knew just the thing to do. She ordered them some sandwiches and juice to be delivered to the room. Peter and Adam took their backpacks to their area and looked at some maps that they reviewed with their dad. They decided that perhaps the best place to go first was to take a day trip to see the 'Great Wall of China' with the entire family as neither Sam nor Kate had done any sightseeing. They could charter it through the hotel.

Adam still complained of a slight buzzing and could not figure out what was the cause of it. As he was tired though, he fell asleep. Then it was lights out for all of them.

In the morning after breakfast, Brad called his brother, Sam, to set up the day schedule. Between the two of them, it was decided on the half day tour to the 'Great Wall of China' called the 'Badaling Tour.' They could be picked up at the hotel, do the tour and be back early in the day for dinner plans. It would give them a chance to spend time in the hotel around the pool and give the children a chance to swim in the pool area.

The tours they researched depended on personal interest and budget. Sam, Kate, and Allie met the rest of the family at the hotel to begin the tour. Though excitement was high for each family member, there was some apprehension regarding what to expect and what to prepare for. The tour guide, a small Chinese girl with pitch black hair cut in neck length and a full set of bangs, provided some history as they traveled to the site where this tour begins. She introduced herself then began to tell them that the wall was built in sections overlapping each other that was the same as the section around Beijing. The purpose was to keep out invading tribes.

Called 'The Wall of Ten Thousand Li' with li being a Chinese measurement and equal to one-third of a mile. It winds over mountains and valleys. Built entirely by hand using earth, brick and stone, it stands about 25 feet high with towers from 35 to 40 feet high spaced about 300 yards apart. The top is paved with bricks set in lime to withstand the hoofs of horses and horsemen. The structure is one of the great wonders of the world. Everyone gasped as she added that some sections of the wall date to between the 8th and 5th centuries BC on through the 14th century. She added that near the tourist centers, the wall is being preserved and renovated as some locations are in disrepair and are prone to graffiti and vandalism.

The guide was speaking in different languages to accommodate the varied tourists on the tour. One little girl asked her if there was a chance that she could fall off the top with the guide assuring her that it was safe and not to worry about that but instead enjoy the sight of it. She advised them the tour would be about three hours long.

They also were able to tour the 13 Ming Tombs of Chinese Imperialists well over 500 years of age. By this time, the group was tiring and happy to return to the hotel. They were glad that they had decided that they should spend the evening around the water park and pool area swimming, eating pizza, and visiting. They had so much to catch up and to call Grandpa and Grandma on Skype. They learned that there was plenty of rain at home so the gardens and yard were wet. The pets were fine also. Allie got a chance to ask her sister, Emilee, how her kitten, McCarthy, was doing.

Chinese Pagoda

It also gave them some time to review what to see and when. They all knew the days would go by so quickly. Since Sam had some classes and appointments for the next day, Brad suggested they do the Olympic Center and the Birds Nest. They could get a tour guide from the hotel and that would allow them an opportunity to see some of Beijing. Kate and Allie decided they would join them in the morning. Sam thought he would like to have them tour the university the following day then they could make plans to visit the girls' pen pal in Zhengzhou. They also spoke of seeing some Panda Bears but left that for later on. Allie and Abby had a pamphlet on the bears. They read some information to the interested listeners. The girls said, "They look so cute. See the baby bear. They are in a wildlife center in Southwest China in a province called Sichuan. There are only about 1600 left in the wild so the center that houses them is critical to their survival." The dads looked at each other shaking their heads and wondering if a visit there was even possible but didn't say anything.

Panda Bear

CHAPTER 5

A Strange Day in a Foreign Country

The request was granted by the hotel with glee. They offered an elderly gentleman that was without a doubt suited for the American family.

Chen was an invaluable asset to the hotel during the 2008 Olympics in translations as he has relatives that live in many different parts of the world and have taught him their languages, customs, and cultures. Brad chartered a vehicle and piled his family into the van to see Beijing for a day. He asked each of them what they specifically would be interested in and made a note to fulfill each request. He was in high spirits.

Chen fit right in with them as he enjoyed the young children seeing his city for the first time as he started with explaining that Beijing was often referred to as Peking. The city is the capital of the People's Republic of China and probably could be noted as one of the most populated cities in the world. Nate could not believe this and asked, "In the whole world?"

Chen replied, "It is so and, in fact, it is the second largest city in China only next to Shanghai. I am so proud of our city as it is the center of China's political, cultural, and educational center." He went on to ask the children what they thought of the airport as it hooks up to the network of high speed rail systems and highways. But Chen reminded them of the history that goes back three millennia. He added, "I was once told that the earliest findings of habitation was in the caves of Dragon Bone Hill dating back more than 230,000 years ago. It has seen many a dynasty rise and fall.

We do have a problem with air quality due to pollution. I am certain the hotel mentioned that during the 2008 Olympics, there was a great number of air improvements tactics such as closing factories, shutting down industry, limiting traffic, and more.

We also get dust from the erosion of the deserts in northern China.

Beijing has rivers which are all tributaries in the Hai River system and has the Grand Canal and South-North Water Transfer Project. I tell you this as on a periodic basis the dams are opened to clear the silt out of the rivers. It is a wondrous and exciting time to see the huge movement of water shooting high in the sky. It would be a sight that you all would never forget. Now for today, I would believe that the Olympic Center would be an excellent place to start. I recall every detail of the 2008 Olympics with the people who participated and those that watched. There is the Bird's Nest, the Water Cube and the National Aquatics Center where Michael Phelps became so famous. I will show you the Beijing National Stadium which I referred to as the

Bird's Nest. It is known as a formal arena for athletic events but it evolved into a place to meet the needs and desires of ordinary people. It hosts a children's experimental center with thousands of children participating in daily events. Many tourists come to see the building. The Water Cube has become a popular destination as an aquatic wonderland with a wave pool, water slides, a marine environment and many more. So lets go see these places and make it a day to remember for your family." Which is exactly what happened.

The morning flew by for the parents Brad, Susan, and Kate. The children were all in awe of what they saw. They listened to Chen as he told them about events that took place and what is happening now.

It was later in the afternoon that Chen showed them an excellent open area to eat lunch. It was a completely different experience as there were individual booths that served choices not common to anyone but Chen. He helped each one of them pick out what he thought they would like and munch on as they walked through the area.

Brad whispered to Susan, "How could we have been so lucky to get a person like Chen to show us how the Chinese live and what they eat."

She shook her head in agreement. Peter and Adam came close to their parents telling them that Yuan was seen following them. He tried to appear incognito but both boys recognized him. Brad became alarmed as he heard that they had met in the San Francisco Airport, then at the Beijing Airport and now here. He became suspicious and spoke to Chen about it. He asked Chen, "What do think is going on here that he would be following us?" Chen slowly reacted as he was thoughtful in his response saying that perhaps he was hired by the municipal government that is regulated by the local Communist Party of China.

He also thought it was strange to pick out a common family from America to track and follow them. He cautioned Brad that they should only act as a family and there probably wasn't much to worry about.

They turned their attention to the marketplace and did some shopping.

The incident was quickly forgotten. Abby and Allie wanted to find something for Sadako that she could use. Chen, Susan, and Kate looked the items over to give some directions to the girls. They finally chose a pencil box that had inscriptions on it.

It was getting late but Brad mentioned to Chen that while ships were carrying goods to America and Europe, at the same time there were ships carrying old electronic equipment back to China. He told Chen that he and his dad had watched a program that called China an 'electronic wastebasket of the world'. Chen agreed and said that even close by there were dump sites where people were cleaning the minerals from the parts. Brad asked Chen that while the rest of the family was shopping could he show him a site like this to affirm this for his dad who was an environmentalist.

Chen slowly let out his breath through his long white beard, took off his hat, rubbed his head, then agreed. It was only blocks away behind a fence. The family hardly noticed that they were gone as they were excited about the marketplace. Abby turned to ask her dad a question then noticed that both he and Chen were not in view.

She called to her mom who also became concerned. In the meantime, Brad was viewing the stockpile. He took out his Iphone, took a picture, and sent it to his dad's e-mail address. He noticed that Chen was not to be seen. He started towards the marketplace when he was arrested for using the Internet without permission. The officer explained that there is a great firewall and vast censorship apparatus to make it difficult to get on line. The officer hand cuffed Brad and took him to Central Headquarters. There he saw Yuan who had been following them. He smirked at Brad and slouched off.

Meanwhile back at the marketplace, Susan and Kate were left unaware of what had happened. They were afraid as neither Brad nor Chen were anywhere in sight. Kate called Sam to get some direction about what to do. He told them to call a taxi to take them back to the hotel. He would meet them there to sort this out.

Meanwhile, back at Central Headquarters, a translator was assigned to Brad to ensure that his story was correctly translated to the officials.

All that Brad could think of was why he did this. He was shocked at himself, especially since Chen had advised him to act like a family and they would be safe. Brad realized he was in a foreign country under a whole different government than he was familiar with. He asked for someone from the American Embassy to come to his assistance. He was terribly distraught at where his family was at and how he betrayed their trust in him. Even Chen left him as he lived here and knew the political climate and restrictions.

The officials would not let him use a phone after he had requested to call his family. It took about an hour before the Embassy official arrived.

Brad explained who he was and why he was being detained. After some discussions with the Chinese officials, they agreed that the pictures did not go through and Brad was freed to go. They did keep his phone though and urged the Embassy to stress that he was being watched closely. The Embassy Official gave him a ride back to the hotel to Brad's relief. He couldn't thank him enough and promised that this was out of character for himself and there would be no further incidents.

As he walked through the lobby, Sam was coming out of the elevator.

Brad shamefully told him what he had done and what had happened.

Brad said, "Sam, I am sick to my stomach for what happened. We had such a good day and good time. We had a cheerful gent as our tour guide who showed us so many different places. Then I thought of how dad might like to see what the electronic trash pile looks like. He and I watched this program on public television with both of us so disgusted with it all and here it was for real. I didn't even think of censorship. The Embassy came to my assistance and all is well. I don't even know what to tell the family. I even wonder if this will affect your relation with the university. I left my family in a lurch. Thanks for being here to calm them as they have no idea where I went. Even Chen abandoned us knowing that we were being followed. I saw that guy that the boys and Susan told me about. I wonder how he is tracking us? Lets go check our luggage." Sam gave him a pat on the back and told him that it sounded like this was serious and agreed to the search. They entered the elevator and headed to the suite. The family was so thankful to see him and Susan shed a few tears in relief. Allie and Abby ran to their dads and jumped into their arms telling them each that they were the best dads in the world.

He told them what a stupid thing he had done and what happened. He explained that it was a spur of the moment decision and he was exonerated but they kept his cell phone. He told them about seeing Yuan there smirking at him. Then they searched the bags and found the disc in Peter's backpack. They wrapped it in tin foil to destroy its ability send out a message. Adam opened his eyes wide open and said, "The sound is gone. It was really bugging me. Here there was a bug bugging me!" Brad assured his family that he would be mindful of where he was and the consequences that could result.

They ordered in some food to console and celebrate. Sam said, "Tomorrow I will be with you to make sure of that. It used to be me that acted on the spur of the moment and you were the cautious type. I have plans to tour the Peking University and look at some gardens that will take your breath away. Then we will begin the planning to go to the girls' pen pal city. I am not sure how to accomplish that yet but we will make it work."

CHAPTER 6

Peking University Tour

The next day Sam sent a University Service to pick up the family and bring them to the campus. The student driver described some of the sights along the way then dropped them off at the cottage where Sam and Kate were staying. With some apprehension Brad and Susan were a bit taken aback as they had pictured a small two room kitchenette. Instead here was what appeared to look like a small palace with traditional Chinese landscaping. They knocked and were even more surprised by the interior decorations. Susan said, "I could live like this any day of the week." Kate nodded and adding, "I expected a small dorm structure in the beginning. We were both pleasantly surprised. I have a whole new respect for this country and the people."

Sam had some goodies, coffee, and drinks set out for them. Abby and Allie disappeared into Allie's room to spend some time together. Sam showed them to the sitting room that stunned them as well with the paintings on the walls. After some chit chat, Sam offered that his workplace/lab is in the Life Sciences building. He added that Brad along with the boys would be interested in getting a firsthand description of the progress in the experiments begun by a lone Austrian professor who showed that bees are not color blind but that they have a definite color sense except for the color red. He searched for the method that bees use to communicate by watching them through a glass plate. Sure enough, he observed the dance of the bees. It is the circling dance and the wagging dance to differentiate whether they had nectar or pollen. Wow!

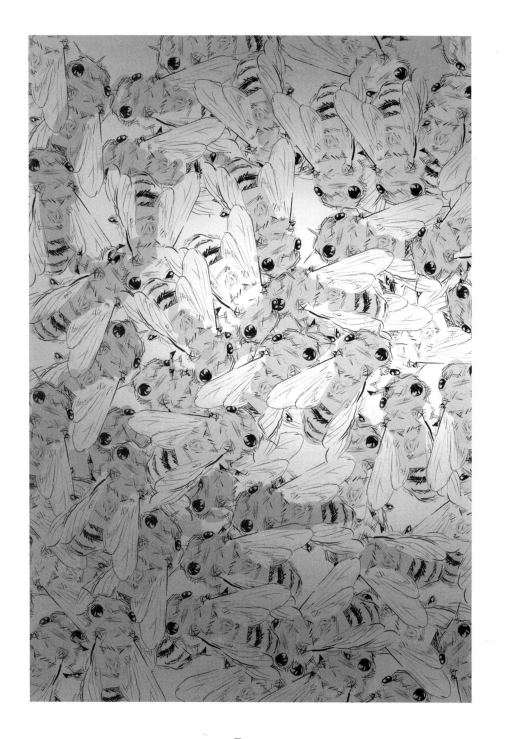

Bees

Can you imagine his insight into this decades ago? Because this is a global problem, our group is utilizing what those before us ascertained and how that can be intertwined with what other scientists have learned.

For me, I am studying the effects of pesticides especially neonicotinoid insecticides. We are making progress for sure. Nate, Peter, and Adam will be interested in our studies. Susan could stay here with Kate as they have not had much time together. When we return, we can tour the campus and I will fill you in with some history about this institution.

How about it, guys?" They all agreed and off they went to the lab and promised to be back in about an hour and a half.

Susan admitted to Kate that she had surmised that she would be lonesome here with no friends. Kate told her that she had little time to visit as she was gathering information on China's Catholics as they are split between those loyal to the Vatican and those who worship under the state sanctioned church. She planned to write a synopsis on her observations.

She added that there is social pressure that change is needed toward the people of faith. Kate then said, "Now tell me all that has been happening and how you dealt with Brad, Peter and Adam on their trip to Peru.

I was so grateful that you took such good care of Allie. She will miss your place with the boys and Abby. With you coming here, our tasks here will be made easier. I miss all of you as well. You helped so much by bringing Allie to us. Of course, this will change my schedule some but I will adjust. Actually between you and me, I kind of have a sense that we will be home by Christmas. Emilee will be anxious to celebrate Christmas with us as well."

Susan and Kate talked the whole time filling each other in on each other's events and happenings plus some gossip. It seemed that the guys came back too soon. They did agree that Abby and Allie could stay behind if they so chose while they walked around the grounds.

While they were strolling, they spoke of the birthday party with cake and candles for the girls. They do not know anything so it will be a surprise.

Nate liked that saying, "Yummy! The cake will be good."

Sam led them on the tour telling them that the Peking University was founded in the late 1890s and has educated some of the most prominent modern Chinese leaders. The university is a national institution with some 30 colleges and 12 departments. It is a leader in basic science research and teaching with 216 research institutions and centers along with the largest library of its kind in Asia. He said, "I am so privileged by the opportunity to study here as well as is Kate." Then went on telling them that at one time the campus was located north of the Forbidden City in Beijing. Now the campus is near the Summer Palace and the old Summer Palace which is an area where many of the famous gardens and palaces were built. We are approaching Weiming Lake with walking paths and small gardens. They walked over a stone bridge that led to houses, pagodas, and historical buildings. They turned and walked back to the "cottage" and were filled with wonder at the architectural marvels.

Kate and Sam prepared and served them a delicious meal of creamed vegetables on a bed of rice. They spoke of what are some favored foods and talked about the tasty morsels from the marketplace yesterday.

Brad broke in shaking his head, "I have such bad memories of what happened. It was irrational. All I could think about was the poorest of poor people cleaning out uranium and other strange metals out of the old computers from America and other countries. I wanted Dad to see that the story was real so I tried to send a photo. Of course it didn't go through as there is a censorship here. Now I wonder if they are going to watch me very closely even though they have my cell phone." Sam brought the subject back to food by mentioning that a favorite is Peking Roast Duck. He added that he and Kate do not leave the campus as time is so precious to study and they live on a restricted budget.

The boys wanted to get back to the hotel to do some water park activities and swimming. Allie asked if Abby could sleep over for the night. It was given an okay as long as she brushed her teeth. As she and Allie were about the same size, clothes would not be an issue. They giggled and asked to be excused.

It was a good time to announce that this is a celebration of birthdays for Abby and Allie. "We are a bit late but the old saying goes, 'Better Late Than Never,' said Sam. The girls were so surprised when the candles were lit on the cake. Nate led them in singing, 'Happy Birthday' in his clear and resonant voice. He then said, "Now can we eat the cake?" They all agreed and enjoyed both the cake and watching the girls open their gifts. Allie and Abby mentioned that at last year's party who would have thought that the next one would be in China!

Sam did broach the subject that tomorrow he had planned to take the family to downtown Beijing to view some museums. There is so much history that none of us know about so I did some reading. There are more than100 museums in Beijing. Then located at the outskirts close to where we were some days ago are Thirteen Tombs of the Ming and Qing Dynasties. I know you have heard me mention the Forbidden City which is the former residence of the emperors of China. It lies at the historic heart of Beijing. It is said that within it, there are treasures of nearly 2,000 years as the Imperial Capital with its lush pavilions and gardens. He asked Brad about wanting to avoid downtown Beijing.

Brad did put his lips together and shook his head. He added," I will think about it and let you know tomorrow. There are so few days and I know how you are giving up a lot of work time for us"

Sam nodded then said, "But look what you have done for us. Kate and I are so grateful that you personally assisted us in getting Allie over here. There are museums on Marco Polo, inventions of early Chinese, the canals, and the list goes on but lets just see. We could spend part of the day sightseeing some things without going to the center of the city. The following day we should go to see Sadako. I have studied the route and if we take the train, it will take too long so I am suggesting the high speed rail which will take about 2 hours each way. We will need to get to their village which is rather remote. Perhaps you could check with the hotel on a recommendation. Enough already, these boys are getting antsy to get to the pool. I will call the car to take you back to the hotel. It has been a wonderful day for all of us. Not too much excitement but just being together was so good for all of us."

Later on, Brad called Sam to tell him that the hotel had a transport service in Zhengzhou that could take us to the village but they strongly urge us to stay overnight. They are so helpful here and offered to find us a place there. They suggest that we leave about 10:00 tomorrow morning to take the high speed rail. Their service will pick us up and take us to their hotel in that city to check in and then drive us to the village to visit. The car would stay with us while we visit for a fee of course. Then return us to the hotel to come back to Beijing via regular train which is about five hours but at a much lower cost. The hotel suggested visiting the Shaolin Temple which is not only known as one of China's important Buddhist shrines but also as the ancient center of Chinese Kung-fu which would give the boys a real eye opener." He added, "That would take us to the day when we have our reservations to fly back to America."

Sam slowly acknowledged what he heard and agreed. He asked, "What about the hotel room in Beijing?" Brad responded that the hotel will transfer our lodging to their hotel in Zhenzhou so there will not be double charges. Sam said, "Wow, we picked a great place for you to stay. But I am already melancholy about thinking of you leaving. Kate and I have discussed that we think we will have enough research that we could come home in time for Christmas and I will be happy about that.

We will talk in the morning. Good night, Bro."

Chapter 7

Round Trip Beijing to Zhengzhou Via Trains

The families met at the rail station to begin a trip that none of them could even imagine what would take place. It was about 9:30 in the morning allowing them ample time to find the car they were assigned to. The whole train looked like something out of a science fiction movie. The Zhengzhou-Xi'a speed rail that was aero-dynamically designed. It was silver with a red streak along the bottom close to the rail, had many windows, and was nearly soundless.

Abby and Allie were amazed at the beauty of the car that they were assigned to and felt comfortable boarding it. Following them the rest of the family located their seats and soon it was moving so smoothly that none of them realized that it had started. The children grouped into one area began to look at some maps they had picked up in the station. Since none of them had any electronic equipment, they entertained each other by looking at how the landscape changed as they whispered through the countryside.

They learned that Zhengzhow is pronounced 'Chengchow'. The map showed that the city lies on the southern bank of the Yellow River. Allie and Abby wondered how they were going to converse with Sadako's family wondering if any of them could translate what each other was saying.

Close by the parents were making some plans of their own as there would not be any sort of guide for them and they realized they were tackling an unknown part of China with no knowledge of where the pen pal, Sadako, and her family lived. They committed to being vigilant to safe guard their children and themselves. Brad had looked up the city on the computer to get some statistics telling them that the city serves as the major transportation hub for central China. Surely there were people who could interpret for them. They spoke of how important this was for their daughters to meet and spend some time together with Sadako. So they nodded in agreement that it would work out and they could depend on the transport service that the hotel was renting for them. This added suspense to the adventure.

It was a sunny day with the expected temperature to be 85 degrees Fahrenheit. It picked up the excitement for each of them. Their conversation turned to the differences in the culture in China. Sam told them that he has read some of the history. He spoke saying, "As a society, it is primarily agrarian yet much of what is distinctive had been developed in Chinese cities. It would take years to understand the effect of the dynasties, the invasions and the political systems. There is a remarkable sense of continuity. There is little similarity to our country as our culture is completely different. This makes for interesting study."

Kate added that in her study of religion she looked at the evolution of Chinese writing. Though difficult to learn, Chinese writing with its more than 10,000 numbers and letters is lovely to behold. Chinese characters represent objects as it is depicted in an abstract form. She told them that she had read somewhere that Roman's characters represent a sound in spoken words while the Chinese made their letters flowing. Then Sam told them that the Chinese were great inventors from 400 to 200 B.C. They invented the cross bow, the kite, and the magnetic compass followed by paper and even the wheel barrow. I saw how they began using block printing. We know what we like to use on the 4th of July is fireworks. They were invented by the Chinese as well as gun powder and list goes on. The world did not get to see much of what they had done until Marco Polo brought them back to Venice, images of their art, poetry, and paintings.

The children called back to them that they were entering the terminal for Zhengzhou. The trip went so fast. It was most enjoyable with no rumbling of trains or hearing the click-clack of the traditional train they were used to.

As they departed the car, the parents cautioned the children to be buddies with each other as there were so many people. Brad looked for the van driver who was to be holding a card with their names on it. It took some doing to get through the crowds as they had several suit cases to carry with them. At least there was no need to use any facilities in the terminal and the children helped in searching for their driver. Then Nate called out, "There he is!" The young man was about 25 years of age and got a big smile on his face when they waved to him. He called out that he would come to help them. He spoke broken English so they were optimistic that all would be well. He helped them along with the bags into the vehicle telling them that he had grown up in this city and delivered packages for an international company for many years that included a huge poultry factory that was located in the area probably close to the family they were to visit. So off they went in search of Abby and Allie's pen pal who lived in a rural area. He said, "Call me Li. I will stay with you during your visit and take you to our hotel later this afternoon or early evening. I learned how to speak your language from a missionary who in turn wanted to learn how to write Chinese. It was an easy trade-off."

He asked the family where they were from in America and soon the children were jabbering with him. Adam asked him why China is called the 'Land of the Dragon' as in our stories dragons are demons. In our country, we have 'Uncle Sam.' Li replied, "Chinese legends portray that dragons are divine animals that help people. It was believed then and still is now that the dragon is a mythical, divine creature bringing greatness, goodness and blessing. Does that help you understand?" They all said "Yes" in unison.

He seemed to know where to go on the highway and kept giving them information. Abby and Allie asked about the Panda bears and where they live in the wild. He told them that it was in another province in a reserve where they are protected. They murmured that it would be a thrill to see them.

As Li watched the signs on the roads, he heard that the family might like to visit the best known tourist attraction, the Shaolin Temple, which is one of China's important Buddhist shrines and is the ancient center of Chinese Kung-fu. Sam nodded that they would see how tomorrow went as there were some temples and museums closer in as they had to get back to Beijing.

As they drove through a smaller community, he spotted a pagoda and asked if the family had toured one yet. Sam told him that they had not but it looked to be a possibility in the days ahead. Li then told them though there are pagodas in many Asian countries, the Chinese pagoda which is constructed as a memorial is usually eight sided with odd shaped stories. They are built mostly of wood but have brick, glazed tile and porcelain decorations. It was a sight to see.

Li turned his attention to study a road sign then nodded that it seemed familiar.

Meanwhile the two couples were whispering among themselves that Li was the answer to interpret what Sadako's family was saying. Sam cleared his throat and asked Li if he would do a favor for them. Li then listened asked, "What would you like me to do?" Sam asked him if he would interpret to them what the

Chinese family would say as they agreed that he would be perfect for this. Li sort of startled and said, "Sure, I can do that. I have to ask though what would you have done without me?" Sam said, "We are not certain so we are very appreciative of the assistance." Li looked left and then right nodded that Sadako's house was nearby and asked if she had given them a clue. Allie and Abby chimed in that Sadako wrote that their house is the yellow one. With that, Li turned and pulled up to the house.

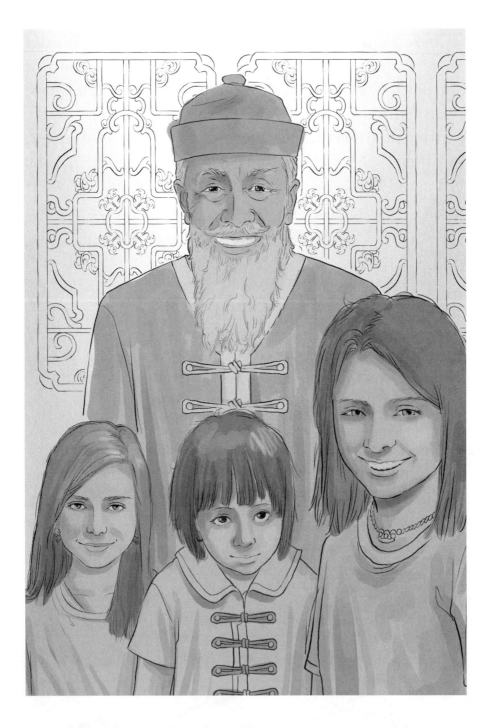

Two American Girls and Chinese Pen Pal With Her Grandfather

The family inside came outside to greet their guests. There was grandpa, grandma, mom, dad and Sadako all smiles. They bowed to invite them inside. Li spoke first to ask if anyone spoke English. They all shook their heads sideways indicating no. He continued on then to introduce Sam, Kate, and Allie as one family then Brad, Susan, Peter, Adam, Abby, and Nate.

Sadako took the girls' hands and led them to her room. Sadako's family seemed a bit overwhelmed with so many people but soon relaxed and invited them into the sitting room. Susan and Kate looked around then motioned if they could go to the kitchen with the ladies. The cooking of food permeated the whole house. Kate made a hand motion to ask if they could help with the food and setting out plates. She was hungry and was certain that the rest of the family was hungry as well. She sort of moved her hand across the front of her face, smiled, and nodded to tell them that the smell was so good. The two ladies smiled and nodded as well then gave them small bowls. They motioned that the table was small but everyone could come to sit down for Miso which is a soup in China. It didn't take long for the guys and boys to find a place to sit. Nate noted that he was so hungry. The girls were served soup in Sadako's room that was almost never heard of but the ladies thought it was best for space. The girls all giggled and took the bowls.

Li kept up a running monologue to keep the families in touch with each other. He was last to sit down and enjoyed the soup. The next serving was steamed chicken pieces with vegetables on rice. It was so flavorful. Sadako's mom and grandma beamed with pleasure. After everyone was full, they motioned to go outside to the garden to see the many plants and the special garlic. The girls' joined the family as they walked around the garden.

The grandpa was so kind looking with his long white hair tied in a pony tail and a white beard. He was small in stature and smiled often. He began by telling them that he had lived here all his life and was happy to be where he is. He welcomed the family from America that he did not know much about. Mostly they stayed close to home as they liked life to be slow. The city center was too much noise and commotion.

He told them that they grew their own vegetables and catch fish in the river. It is cold in the winter and hot in the summer. We are not in the path of the big dust storms that blow from the desert to the northwest of us. We feel blessed and with that he folded his two hands together and shut his eyes for a moment. Then he smiled and looked around saying, "We look forward to the celebration of New Year with fireworks and good times." Sadako whispered something to him and his eyes grew wide. He said, "I will tell you a story about three Chinese brothers named One, Two and Three with Three being the youngest. It is a story about the New Year in China." Sadako was smiling as she listened to her grandfather tell her favorite story with Li repeating it in English. The grandfather went on to say,

"It was the most magic time of all they year. The three boys were anxious of what their surprise would be in the morning. They were certain that they were getting a new toy. That did happen. Their mom introduced them to a huge lantern in the shape of a dragon." As the grandfather told the story, suddenly there was a loud explosion which filled them all with fear and apprehension to what happened.

Sadako's grandfather froze as he said, "It must be an explosion in the poultry factory up the road. We must hurry to see if they need help." Li piled them all in the van and off they sped.

By the time they arrived, they could see fire sweeping through the processing plant with injured, burned workers crawling out of the rubble. Li asked Grandpa if he knew how many workers there were on each shift. Grandpa told him that usually about three hundred workers per shift. Brad looked as his sons and motioned if they could detect where the workers were. Peter and Adam said they could sense that many were trapped. Brad asked Li to ask a supervisor if he had a bobcat available for use as he knew how to run it. The supervisor nodded and took them to a garage. The women asked Sam to see if they could assist with first aid. Li then spoke with the supervisor who got blankets, kits, and bottles of water for the injured. Everyone chipped in to help and if nothing else to console those who were panicked by the disaster. Even the children helped to carry water bottles around and hold people's hands.

Brad started up the bobcat and asked the boys where he should begin the task of opening up a wall. For a moment they stared at the structure and then pointed. Sam was coming around the corner observing what he had just seen. Brad then started the effort of opening the corner where there were the most workers huddled and unable to get out. There was no exit close to them. Piece by piece the wall came apart and out tumbled hundreds of people grateful to be free.

By now the fire trucks came and set up to distinguish the flames. Sam asked Li to ask the supervisor if he had a checklist of the names of the shift workers. Li reported back that he did. Sam and Li started to ask for people's names and if the workers that were not burned could help in identifying them. More workers kept streaming out of the plant most of them coughing and trying to breathe in fresh air.

It did not take too long before CCTV was on the scene followed close with the Beijing Evening Newspaper. Reporters were snapping pictures of the disaster, the workers, and the rescuers.

Brad then stopped the machine to speak with Peter and Adam. He asked them if they could sense anymore places that he should attempt to break into. As ambulances streamed into the work yard, the boys looked at each other and using all their special senses focused on the second floor. They pointed to the place where there was a stairway and a door. It was too high for the bobcat so Brad went in search of the firefighter with a ladder on the truck. Evidently the door was an exit but it must have jammed shut.

The fire truck came around the side and extended the ladder to the top and climbed up. Using axes they broke down the door releasing many workers who could hardly breathe with the heavy smoke. No one was burned though and they were climbing down the ladder and the stairs.

What seemed like hours later, all the workers were accounted for with most of them getting checked for smoke inhalations and burns which were superficial. The supervisor was also breathing heavy as he came around to thank the families for all they did and the lives they saved. Of course, this was all translated by Li. Each of them had blackened hands, red eyes, and smelled of smoke.

It was decided that Sadako and her family would be taken home by a neighbor as Brad and Sam wanted to get back to Zhengzhou. Abby, Allie, and Sadako made a circle with their arms and hummed a tune.

Language was no barrier as each believed that a bond of friendship with each other was there. Li called out that the van was ready to go. As they were getting into the van, a reporter came by to get a photo and a statement from the families. Sam said, "We did what we had to do and are grateful that no one was seriously injured." The reporter commented that they were tourists from America and this is a story that I cannot pass on. "I must get some details as this will go all over

China," he said. Brad said they were exhausted and asked Li if he could give them a number they could be reached at the hotel. The reporter told them that he would come by later to get their version.

The family was quiet on the way back to the city. Sam especially as he kind of suspected that his nephews were instrumental in saving many lives but he kept quiet. Li took them to the hotel for check-in and advised the front desk of what had happened. They all looked in awe at this family and some even shed tears for what they had done. The hotel management ordered a special suite and plenty of food to go around.

The reporter did come back and was allowed to do his story about the American family that came to visit a pen pal resulted in saving hundreds of lives with their quick action and aid to the victims. He told them that the story has gone global.

Brad was not about to say anything of the gift of special senses that his boys had received last year. He lay down and remembered how the boys had gone to foothills close to their home to target practice. Due to disorientation, they got lost. Both for warmth and safety, they built a campfire that set the woods on fire isolating them in a cave. Searching for food and water, they came upon a UFO and two aliens that were also isolated inside the mountain. They assisted each other to exit but before leaving earth, the aliens beamed a special light into each of his sons' eyes. He had to keep this silent and wondered if anyone had noticed.

The families were too tired to shower or clean up. They each found a place to lay down and fell asleep.

The next morning there was no sightseeing as there were reporters all over the hotel. The family decided to board their train to get to Beijing. That was not to be as the City of Zhengzhou had prepared a special ceremony for both families. In addition, they brought Sadako and her family to the hotel. The Mayor of Zhengzhou presented each person a memento of the city with a design signifying the heroic efforts that each of the families had given. It was a miracle story. Reporters from all around the world were there snapping photos and asking questions. Li became a Chinese hero for his part in the rescue.

Sam called his dad to tune in to any television station to watch what was happening in China. Of course the three girls were most delighted that they got another chance to see each other. Attending were many of the factory workers whose lives were saved by the 'bobcater' and his family from America.

It seemed like hours of speeches and remarks before the crowd began to disperse. The train had been held up to accommodate the ceremony and were so pleased to have been chosen as the carrier of these special people from America. The hardest part was boarding the train and settling for a five hour ride back to Beijing.

The conductor provided a special car in order that there would be privacy to clean themselves and change out of the blackened, smeared clothes they were wearing. Kate and Susan took the children into the shower room searching through the luggage to find some clean clothes. Brad and Sam studied the menu and couldn't really decipher it. They asked the conductor to bring them rice, vegetables, and some dessert along with beverages. Then Sam and Brad assessed the situation revisiting what had happened. Sam looked at Brad and spoke of observing that Peter and Adam were most helpful in locating the stranded workers. He said, "They appeared to have some special sight to where to begin rescue efforts." Brad tried to minimize what Sam had seen then changed his mind and shared the story about the six days inside the mountain, the aliens they encountered, the morse code as a means to communicate and then how they helped each other exit the mountain. Before they left, they beamed a ray into the brothers' eyes. For a long time they knew something was different. They did not speak about it though. They told me after they saved us in the Amazon country. First they saved themselves in the mountain, then Mannie, myself and themselves, now all those hundreds of people. I am so proud of them but made a decision not to tell anyone even Susan in order for them to grow up as regular teenagers. I would ask that same pledge from you. Sam agreed with his brother that this should be kept silent until they could grow up and can make their own decisions.

Then it was their turn to shower before the food was served. They were hungry as bears but waited for the whole family to say a prayer of blessing. After they nearly had consumed all the food, Allie and Abby brought up a new subject not related to the disaster. They mentioned that a gift should be purchased for Grandpa and Grandma from the families.

They suggested that for Grandma, they could look for a pin such as the plumed peacock. For Grandpa, they looked around with Adam saying that Grandpa liked puzzles that were made of metal such as two horseshoes that needed to be twisted and turned to come apart. Or a dragon statue to match the one that he already had but this would be authentic from China. Allie also wanted to purchase a silk scarf for her sister, Emilee, and send back to the states with Abby.

They all decided they would look in the gift shop at the hotel later on. The children offered to choose the items and asked the dads to pay for them. For awhile, they laid their heads against the seats and napped until the conductor came to tell them that they were entering Beijing. Sam and Kate decided to come to the hotel for several hours. They were all realizing that tomorrow was departure day to return to the United States.

As they were checking in at the Beijing Hotel, a staff member came to deliver a package for Brad. He was stunned as he opened it to find in it was his Iphone with a note of apology from the Central Government.

They were proud to acknowledge the contribution that Brad and the families had played in saving hundreds of Chinese lives in the disaster at the poultry factory. Brad nearly choked as he read the note aloud.

CHAPTER 8

The Grand Canal and Dragon Boats

The families parted with an agreement to meet for breakfast early in the day to spend time together before departure time at the airport. They knew they would sleep good after the long day and all the events that occurred.

Sure enough there were Sam, Kate, and Allie ready to take them all to breakfast at 8:00 A.M. Sam joked that since they really didn't get to see the Shaolin Temple and the ancient center for the Chinese Kung-fu, he wanted to take them to see the Grand Canal. It is both historic and scenic that would leave them all memories of how the Chinese people live along the river. He asked at the university for some material on the history and how it was built. So they decided this was just what they needed on their last day in Beijing.

Sam offered that the Grand Canal runs 1,100 miles between Beijing and the last city to the south Hangzhou. The brochure he read from told the story of the original canal system that was built by an emperor from the Sui dynasty about 14 centuries ago. Because China's rivers ran west to east, it was a dream to find a way to transport rice in the other directions, he wanted to connect the Yellow River to the Yangtze. It took over a million laborers to dig new channels. Peter and Adam broke in to tell that the story sounded much like the building of the Panama Canal to join the Pacific and Atlantic Oceans. Brad added that on their trip to South America, the pilot took them over the Panama Canal to view the project. Sam said, "Actually you boys are right in that the projects are similar. He went on to read from the material that the barges were handled mostly by soldiers. So lets charter a boat, take a ride and have lunch somewhere along the way." They all chimed in that this was a good idea.

Abby and Allie were interested in the house boats and seeing children playing along the way. Many of the families that live along the river are suppliers for the many boat crews that transport grains, lumber, and food.

They saw people working in gardens, tending flocks of geese, and some were fishing in the river.

Brad and Sam recalled a trip that their mom and dad took to the Grand Canyon that is located in Arizona. Their mom told them they were so impressed with the people who live along the Colorado River and the multiple uses for the water. It sort of matched how the people live along the Grand Canal. It seemed to serve as a cultural exchange. The down side of both rivers is the pollution that is occurring. Both countries, the Chinese and Americans are taking steps to curb the pollution as both of them are more than tourist attractions but main arteries for transporting goods.

They were able to find a restaurant as they turned the boat around that had a sign posted saying 'Peking Roast Duck Served Here.' Finally the family could partake of the famous cuisine. Nate asked if they made McDonald's burgers. They did find some common foods that the children enjoyed as well.

Dragon Boats - Ancient

On the return trip, they ate at a place to view a Dragon Boat. They were used for races along the canal. Abby and Allie looked at each other as they recalled out loud that a friend of theirs had taken a trip to Bemidji, Minnesota to stay at a cabin for several weeks. While they were there, the annual Dragon Boat races were held. It was a big deal with over 50 brightly decorated dragon boats each operated by a team that competed to win with a series of races. The event was huge with tents set up on the water front and teams coming from all over the country to participate.

She said it was such fun to watch the races. She said the boats were so colorful with red, gold, bright blue, orange and green. We could take some pictures here and show them to her when we get home. The whole family agreed that this was a good place to take photos. It had been an excellent day and this seemed the appropriate place to turn around and go back to Beijing.

Then it was time to return to the hotel to gather up the load of luggage and head to the airport. The plane was scheduled to depart at 7:00 P.M. Sam, Kate, and Allie accompanied the family to the Beijing Capital International Airport which took about forty minutes from the hotel. It now boasts of three terminals but it takes more time to search out the right terminal.

CHAPTER 9

Leave Beijing

Here is where Sam, Kate, and Allie left the departing family. It was a sad time with Allie and Abby shedding tears as they hugged each other.

Kate and Susan took some photos to show the grandparents. Brad and Sam had lump in their throats as they said their good byes. Brad told Sam, "We will always remember this trip and the best part was spending time with you. At home, we are so busy that we get little time to really visit. Thanks, Bro." Sam shook his head in agreement telling him that they were coming home in several months. Many wishes for a safe journey home to the USA were spoken. The departing family walked into the security area turning and waving.

In the airport parking lot, Sam, Kate, and Allie were about to leave when Allie asked that they stay to watch the airplane leave. Kate put her arms around her daughter saying, "You will miss them, won't you? I can understand. When we live so close you spend most of your time at their house and the past months, it was a real experience to live with them.

We are so happy to have you back with us and we will see them in several months." Allie had a few tears roll down her cheek as she recalled the letter from Sadako, the trip here and the adventures with both families. She was happy to be back with her mom and dad yet knew it would be different. Her mom would homeschool her until they returned home. She would miss her older sister who was married and lived close to their house. Her sister was taking care of her kitten that she was happy about. The thought of her brought a smile to her face as she pictured her black color, with 4 white paws and a patch of white under her chin. She also was wondering how McCarthy and Cami, her sister's puppy, were getting along.

Airplane Leaving China Airport

Still as she watched the airplane ascend into the sky, her hand went up to wave to Abby. Then she turned to her parents saying, "Now I will be ready for us to go back to our cottage. I just wanted to see them off." Her mom and dad were so proud of their daughter. She had not only grown taller this summer, but her hair had bleached some from the sun making it look reddish and her skin was tanned. She seemed to have matured some also. Sam was sure that Allie would like the big pool at the university.

The three of them could go swimming whenever they wanted to. She had become an avid swimmer. Both of the girls, Allie and Abby liked to swim and did so often at home.

Meanwhile in her window seat, Abby looked down to see if she could spot their car. She put her hand against the window feeling so lonely and sort of knew that Allie was feeling the same way. She remembered the sisterly way they got along and could almost feel like twins. Well, they were almost twins as they were born about a week apart in the same year. Allie was a bit taller and her hair was darker than hers. She wore it in a neck length bob where Abby's hair was longer.

She thought of what it would be like to return home to an empty room. Then she realized how Nate must have felt most of the time when the girls played together. The older brothers were team mates then she and Allie were so close so it left Nate to play by himself. She decided she would change that and include him in her activities at least until Allie came back home.

With that, she opened her Ipad and asked Nate to play some games on it with her. He was happy for sure. She looked over at Adam and Peter who were busy looking at something on their Ipads and wondered what it was about as they spoke to their dad. She concentrated on the Mine Game and smiled at Nate.

Adam and Peter told their dad that they had found an interesting article in the pocket of the seat and looked up some information on it. It was related to the Ring of Fire. "Dad," said Peter, "Remember when we were flying over Mexico with Mannie in the 'Domitila', we told you about attending Boys Scouts Jamboree on the Air with a local amateur 'ham' radio operator, NOFBA, who helped with relaying messages to radio operators in Mexico during the earth quake. Well, in this brochure there is information on the Ring of Fire. It is an area where a large number of earthquakes and volcanoes erupt in a ring around the Pacific Ocean. Take out the brochure and see that it extends from the Andes Mountains in Chile up the coast of South America through Central America, Mexico, United States, Canada, Alaska specifically the Aleutian Islands, across the Pacific Ocean to Russia, Japan, Philippines, Indonesia, New Zealand, and Antarctica." Then Adam added that we read that in 1982, 'El Chichon' erupted in Mexico, with many deaths.

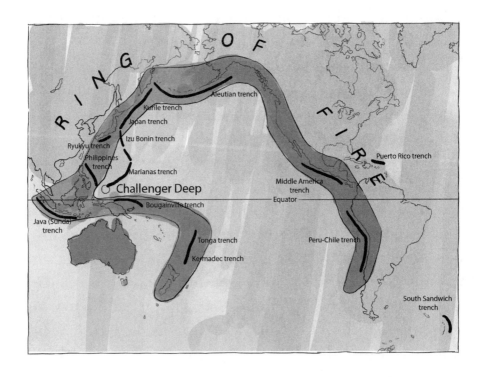

Ring Of Fire

The 'ham' operator at home spoke with 'ham' operators in Mexico to search for relatives and friends. There was a great loss of life during that tragedy. He said, "We sort of felt connected in a way when we read this as these eruptions occur on a regular basis. In our country, there was Mount St. Helens. Alaska holds the record of the second largest earth quake in the world. Wow!" Their dad looked the brochure over then told the boys this was really good information. He did recall the conversation during the flight to Peru. He held up his hand for a moment as the captain came on line after the attendants had completed the spiel about what to do in case of a disaster. No one really paid much attention as it was so repetitive. After all, this was a Boeing 777 Jet Plane with all the safety features built into it. The captain welcomed them all aboard with an excellent weather report and what altitude they were flying at. He spoke of the length of the trip to the San Francisco Airport and the expected time of arrival. He added that with the good weather, they may arrive ahead of schedule. Brad turned his attention to what Adam and Peter were speaking about. He commented that he would study it as his dad spoke often of weather and how it affected the global climate. This might be information he already knew about but it wouldn't hurt to read and remember. The boys went back to their seats happy that their dad had shown interest in the article.

Brad and Susan put their seat backs down while looking at each other smiling. Susan reached out to stroke his cheek feeling quite smug that this whole trip had been a learning experience in addition a safe one.

Brad said, "Now we can relax. The Captain just reported that all is well and we should land on schedule. That is all right with me. I do feel that Sam and I reached a new understanding of each other. This trip was expensive but worthwhile. Just think of what the children learned. You and I never had a chance at something like this. Well, I probably am the one that learned the most. That episode in Beijing could have upset the whole trip with my absurd curiosity. Besides that I knew the censorship restrictions in China. I shudder when I think of what they could have done to me. Thank goodness the ambassador intervened and had me released. Then they sent my phone back. I really needed that. I think I will take a nap. How about you?" He saw that she had beat him to it and was already sleeping.

Six hours into the flight, they were served a light meal of sandwiches, chips, and refreshments. Susan said, "I feel like a new person with the nap I took and now this cup of hot coffee. The children were hungry and now seem more contented. They are busy with their Ipads and games. How are you doing? I haven't asked you lately if you have any remnants of headaches yet?" Brad smiled at her assuring her that he was just fine. They decided to watch a movie.

Just as the movie was ending, Peter and Adam texted their dad to say they felt something strange happening. They wondered if he would check on his Iphone to see if there was any news. He told them not to worry that the Captain would let them know if there was any problem with the airplane. Susan asked him, "What was that about?" He told her the boys asked him to check into his cell phone to get an update on any thing happening. She was a bit puzzled but let it slide.

Eight hours into the flight, the Captain came on line to report that the airplane had lost radio contact with the Control Tower but not to be alarmed. Susan jerked up in her seat and looked her husband straight on, "Brad, what is going on here. I am the mother of the boys and I am getting a sense that there is something you know that I should be told.

It seems odd that Peter and Adam were aware of something happening an hour ago and you dismissed it." He took a deep breath, sort of rolled his eyes and blew out a puff of air saying, "Susan, there is more than you know but I have avoided telling you as it may change the relationship that you have with them. Sam also confronted me at the disaster area at the poultry plant as he observed that the boys have a special sense."

With that he relayed just what he had told Sam. He told Susan that when the boys were inside the mountain a year ago, they encountered a UFO and two outer space aliens also stranded. They learned to trust each other and through morse code they communicated with each other."

With wide eyes, Susan stared at her husband as he filled her in on how the aliens came to overtake the planet earth that looked so green and fresh with plenty of water. They were a superior race and thought they could take over the planet but instead were faced with a military force stronger than they could cope with so they cut a swathe into the mountain. Then they couldn't exit as they could not tolerate the ultra violet rays from the sun when outside of their aircraft. This is where our marvelous children interceded and cut the vines to expose the exit. Before they flew off to return to their homeland, they beamed a ray of energy into our boys' eyes. It was a gift of gratitude. When we were in the Amazon, I learned all about this but thought to protect them for as long as I could so they could learn what this was and how to learn to live with it. Mannie also knew. Our sons kept this secret all winter and only this summer began to speak of it and recognize what it could be used for. The boys told me that often they think that the aliens could foresee the future and this gift could be used for times of dire need.

The gift mesmerized the drug bandits who released us. We would likely have been killed if not for what Peter and Adam did to them. Mannie recognized that right away. He helped the boys with his story telling about the rain forest, the Incas, the mighty Amazon, and the natives that still live off the land.

It gave them the knowledge to built the raft, float the Amazon River, and find the natives to cure me. It is like they can see right through objects. In China, they could sense where the employees were huddled at the exit that was jammed and let me know where to open the wall so they could escape. It was them that saved the people but I tried minimize it to protect them. Can you imagine what would happen if this ever got out to the media before Peter and Adam are mature enough to manage the gift? They told me that at night they can see clearly in the darkness and remember when Adam came to us with his headache. He is especially sensitive to sound as that honing device should not have been heard by the human ear. Sam knows some but he is sworn to secrecy. I try my darndest to treat them like the age they are and respect that someday they will use it for a special purpose. So far they have done a marvelous job of it. I know you will not let it keep you from being the special mom you are now. She couldn't answer. Tears welled up in eyes and Brad put his arm around her to console her. He whispered to her, "We have four marvelous children and it is mostly to your credit. This is so much to comprehend but just as me, it sort of answered some of the questions I had about Peter and Adam. We can never speak of this to them unless they broach it with us. They have each other and so far have succeeded in using the gift to save themselves, Mannie, me and the factory workers. Lets just pretend for now that we have two young teenagers, a curious youngster, a beautiful daughter and each other. I love you and will be forever grateful to those aliens that gave our children this gift." She wiped her eyes, smiled and said, "Now you better check with them on what do they know."

CHAPTER 10

In The Ring of Fire

Brad got up to go the seats where his children were visiting. Peter and Adam were checking on their Ipads and found that there was a 9.6 on the Richter scale earthquake in the Aleutian Islands in Alaska. This meant that there could be a tsunami or tidal wave going to occur somewhere. Brad signaled for the cabin attendant to ask if the Captain was aware of the earthquake and what could follow. She replied that all is being done that can be for now. She added, "The Captain will keep us informed as we approach California which will not be too long now. I would ask that you all remain seated." Sure enough the seat belt warning light came on and Brad returned to his seat. He became alarmed and wondered what would happen to his family and himself. What started out to be a routine flight could very easily turn into a disaster. He recalled how only last year, there was an airplane with over three hundred people crashed while landing. It was chaos with several passengers burned.

His mind envisioned their own airplane sinking into the Pacific Ocean.

He began to wonder that he should have listened to Adam and Peter earlier but decided that would not have changed their flight plan.

The cockpit crew would have had difficulty believing. They would trust destiny now. He texted Peter to ask if he had any more news on his Ipad. Peter returned with this message that San Francisco could expect to have at the least a 7 foot tidal wave. Brad about froze with the news and his thoughts were running amok.

The Captain made an announcement that radio contact had not been restored but other communications could be brought on line to get in contact with the San Francisco Control Tower. He asked all passengers to remain calm and he would announce any updates.

Abby and Nate were scared at what they heard. Nate held onto Abby's hand then told her that God would watch over them all. As his older sister listened, she hugged him and agreed. All the while she knew that they would be facing a challenge with no radio contact and the sea rising. She looked for Adam and Peter noticing that they were busy sketching some curli-cues on a their Ipad. Then texting which she was sure to their dad seated in the row behind herself and Nate. She wondered what they had found but knew her best position would be to keep calm for Nate's sake. She kept him busy playing games and did her level best to speak quietly. It seemed to be working for now.

Meanwhile Peter and Adam asked the cabin attendant to allow them to go to their dad's row of seats to give him some information. She said, "I will allow that but keep very quiet to preserve the calm atmosphere in the cabin. I worry that some one will get scared and scream out loud."

They joined their parents who made room for them. With that, the brothers began to share information with their dad. They learned that though the waves were to be very high, there are low coastal areas to absorb some of the water. They told their dad that the International Space Station would be able to provide information to the affected areas but without a radio contact, it would be useless for the Captain and the aircraft.

So Peter asked his dad if he remembered what he had built as a boy scout called the 'crystal radio'. I have seen it in the basement and studied it while I was a boy scout. Also Adam had studied it once and remembered quite a bit of how to assemble one here. Adam concurred saying, "Crystals have frequencies in them. I think we have all that we need from what we purchased in China for Grandpa and Grandma. We got a necklace with a silk covered wire that we could use for an antenna that would be attached to the crystal. Then for the crystal we could take the one out of the Peacock pin we got for Grandma.

We would need more wire to make a coil but surely some place on this airplane there is a piece of wire. The co-pilot would need to give us his headset. We could transmit to the Control Tower as they know morse code. Peter and I practiced it while we were in the mountain and used it to communicate with our alien friends. At least we could get information to the Control Tower.

I have sketched out the parts and how to assemble them. I am not certain what frequency the transmission would go out on but I am certain the Captain would know that. He may even be able to at least hear back the instructions so we could land. There will be water but this is a large bodied aircraft and at least we would be safe on the ground." Peter then said, "Dad, will you ask to speak with the Captain and get his co-operation?" Brad answered that he would do that immediately and suggested that Susan sit with Nate and Abby to keep them calm.

He put on the light to ask for the cabin attendant to come to their seats. She came, listened and agreed that it was not the best of plans but it was better than no plans. The boys went back to their assigned seats to wait for the response. It took about five minutes and Brad was summoned to the cockpit. In about fifteen minutes, he returned with a nod to the boys that they should join him in the rear of the aircraft where they could build the radio with the help of the cabin attendant. He also told the boys that the Captain is current with his FCC Amateur Radio license and can tap out morse code at 20 words per minute. Adam sort of chuckled to Peter that they wish they could do that.

Susan went into the luggage to locate where the jewelry was. It was not buried too deeply as it had to go through Chinese customs to get it declared so she knew where to look. She pulled out the black velvet cast that held the pin and necklace looking at the beauty of the jewelry then gave it to the cabin attendant.

Other passengers were getting curious and anxiety was building in the area. The cabin attendant asked them to trust that there was a means to communicate that the Captain had mentioned earlier. It settled down the passengers and they watched with interest.

Brad set up a work station in the area that the cabin attendants use for preparing lunches for the passengers. In fact, he chose a small board used to cut cheese on to be the base of the radio. It had been so many years but he forced the technique from the recesses of his mind.

Adam, Peter, and the cabin attendant watched with interest. He took the thin silk covered wire then ran his fingers along it saying to them, "This wire which I am wrapping around the crystal is called the cat-whisker. This is a beautiful crystal and will conduct the radio frequency. The other side of the wire is hooked to the set of head phones." He found a piece of copper wire to use as a ground. For the variometer, he wound a heavier wire 13 turns on a vertical then 30 turns horizontal and finished with 13 more turns to complete the circuit. He asked his sons to look at it and check if it was correctly assembled. They both opened their eyes wide and looked at it. They shook their heads in agreement.

He then tried it out before taking it to the cockpit for the Captain to use. Since the range is only about 25 miles, he was hopeful that there was ship nearby that would pick up the signal and relay to the San Francisco Control Tower. He asked the boys to return to their seats and walked to the cockpit. He asked the

Captain if he could stay there during the use and was given permission. The Captain then began the process of clicking out a message. For awhile there was no response then a submarine that was at close range picked up the signal. There was great excitement building in the cock pit now. The radio man on the submarine relayed the message to the operator at the Control Tower then waited for instructions.

The Control Tower wanted to re-direct the airplane to another airport but the Captain asked for instructions as he would not have enough fuel. They agreed they would need to land in a flooded tarmac. He asked how much water there was on the tarmac and received the message that there was four feet. The Captain asked which runway to use and could they have the directional lights turned on for him to see. They conversed via the radio man on the submarine that they would be ready to land in 32 minutes and could the airport be ready to receive them. The Control Tower would have the fire trucks, boats, ambulances and other emergency vehicles ready to respond should there be an emergency.

With that completed, Brad returned to be with his family leaving the rest of the tasks to the airline employees.

The Captain went on the intercom to begin to relay his message to the passengers that an alternate radio communications had been established and briefly informed the passengers about the earthquake, the tidal wave and the water level on the landing strip at the San Francisco Airport. He went on to add that they need to land due to the fuel supply and all emergency steps have been implemented. He assured the passengers that all that was being done and to listen to the instructions carefully to what the cabin attendant would now repeat for them.

The cabin attendant then gave them instructions on landing which would occur in twenty minutes. She asked each of them to remain calm and step by step gave them confidence that they would survive. A little baby began crying loudly with the mother trying to console it. The other cabin attendant sat next to her to provide assistance on how to help the pressure on the baby's ears. She heated the baby's formula bottle then gave it to the mother which she said the sucking would help the baby. It worked. It seemed as though that was a good omen to many passengers.

The Captain made the announcement that the airplane was close to approaching the landing site and each passenger needed to follow instructions. The cabin attendants took their seats and belted in as well.

CHAPTER 11

Terror On The Airplane

As the huge aircraft slowed its speed, there was great apprehension amongst the passengers, some were crying, others were praying but mostly they were very quiet. Brad kept his family calm and remembered the last time he and two of his sons were caught in the crash of the single engine plane that was sabotaged in the Amazon Rain Forest. The noise had been deafening. This time it was quiet and he tried to keep the panic to a minimum. He and Susan held hands and soothed Nate as he was so young. His blue eyes looked at his dad asking, "Dad, are we going to be crashing. I am afraid." Brad put his arm around his little boy assuring him that they would land safely but there would be a huge splash of water as the airplane would hit the water. He would have liked to have had Abby by his side also. She was allowed to sit with her brothers. He could see they were holding hands as well. Peter and Adam appeared calm. Their dad wondered if they could foresee the future and already knew that they would land safely.

Suddenly the Captain lowered the landing gear and they could hear the sizzle as they touched the top of the flood. Then there was a wall of water that covered the entire airplane. It appeared that the airplane had been swallowed up by the water. As the airplane moved through it, the water slid off and gradually the airplane moved through it.

The Captain had originally planned to park farther from the terminal but the Control Tower instructed him to continue to the building as the passengers could deplane in the hook up with the air step. It worked.

Slowly the airplane moved through the deep water towards the building. Then it stopped. The Captain announced that they had safely landed and were ready to deplane. He thanked them all for the co-operative manner exhibited.

He put his head down on the steering column and let out a big puff of air and relaxed. What an ordeal! He was so thankful for the passenger who knew enough about communications to build the crystal radio.

It sent shivers through him to think of what could have happened then lifted his head in wonder that they had landed without incident. It was like a miracle and he would never forget this as long as he lived. He did have questions in his mind how did that family know when to intervene and how did they know about the events.

With that he rose with shaky legs and fought the nausea that almost hit him. He took several deep breaths then wound his way to the rear of the airplane to thank the crew. They were almost in awe of what had happened and thanked the Captain for the marvelous job of landing this airplane and getting over three hundred passengers and themselves to safety. He shook his head in admiration but inside he was humble as he knew that it wasn't himself but the family who actually saved the airplane. Then he wondered what the media would make of this as he recalled the airplane in the Atlantic Ocean with the Captain that saved all those people. He did not want all that attention.

Then he remembered the radio man on the submarine and wondered if he could ever thank him personally.

As he stepped into the second floor of the terminal, a round of applause and yells greeted him. He was a tall, shy man with whitish hair and a tanned complexion. He wondered if his face would blush with the attention. He walked around thanking the passengers for the calmness exhibited and looked for the family who were the real heroes. Brad caught his eye and shook his head sideways. Then he turned away.

The announcement was made that the luggage would have to be taken off manually as the floor that the luggage usually came in was flooded.

The announcer added that there was an area where coffee, beverages and sandwiches would be offered to the deplaned passengers and the crew. There would be attendants to offer alternate travel arrangements for those who were expecting connecting flights.

Brad and Susan took their children to a quiet area to enjoy the peace they felt to be on the ground without incident. Susan looked into her husband's eyes and nodded. He nodded back. They sat down with the lunch then thanked each of their children for being so patient and trusting. Brad spoke to them of how proud he was of each of them. He gave Abby a big hug then whispered in her ear that what she had done for Nate was appreciated and told her how much he loved her. He gave each of the boys a hug then grabbed Susan for a hug also. Now they could really relax. The food was so good.

They left the children seated while they went to search for a means to get them home. "Home," Susan said, "I will be glad to be home." They spoke with an attendant that offered them a bus trip and that they would offer a free ticket anywhere in the continental USA or a refund.

Brad chose the refund and chuckled as he told the attendant, "We will be happy with a bus ticket to get us home. A refund would be the best option as they had just returned from an expensive trip to China."

She smilingly agreed and that it would take about an hour and a half to make the arrangements. She added that the Captain sent them a special note and a package to thank them for what they did though she didn't know what that was about. She asked them if they would like to have some of their luggage shipped to them or take it with them. Susan thought for a moment than chose to take it with them even if it took a bit longer. Some one would accompany them when the luggage was unloaded.

They returned to their children then opened the package and the card from the Captain. He had enclosed the crystal, the necklace chain and a personal note that he would always remember what they did. It almost choked Brad and Susan but the children were delighted to have the jewelry back that they had picked out for their grandparents. Then Brad remembered he best call them to let them know they were all fine and would be returning on a bus today yet. It would take a day to get them home for sure and asked his dad to call Sam to also let him know the rest of the story about their journey from the Land of The Dragon. He had to remember to ask his dad to meet them at the bus depot as their car was at the airport.

The Land Of The Dragon

Chapter 12

Final Chapter

When the family arrived at the bus depot, Grandpa was there with a big smile on his face. He gave each of them a hug to welcome them home. The children were excited to see that everything was the same.

Brad and Susan were delighted that the countryside was green from the recent rains. Grandpa took them home then drove Brad to the airport to pick up his car. This gave him some time to fill his dad in on the details of the trip, the incident in Beijing with the photo, the fire at the poultry plant and the near disaster with the airplane. His dad sort of scolded him about the photo and the chance he took. Brad told him that the families bonded in China and it was worth it all. As they parted, Brad told his dad that he would see him soon and to tell mom that all was fine.

On the way back, Brad stopped off at the work site to check in. He was amazed at the work accomplished in his absence and complimented the crew. He told them that he would see them the next day. On the way home, he pulled off to a side road, drove to the top of a mesa and got out to take a few minutes to himself.

Brad found a flat rock to sit on and looked out over the scenery below him. He thought of all of the events that happened over the past year. Soon it would be Peter's birthday and wondered what he would like to receive as a gift. Brad remembered last year's gift, the rifle. All this did was bring back a raft of memories. He had an unsettling feeling about how calm Peter and Adam were when the airplane began its descent to the San Francisco Airport.

He thought this is a good time to mull over his feelings before he joined the family. He recalled that even before Peter and Adam told him about the journey in the mountain last August and the aliens that were there, he had questions on their grades and their reserve. He wondered if the aliens had taken over their bodies and could the space ship still be inside the mountain. He shook his head side to side then decided this was not the direction he wanted his thoughts to go. He loved the two boys so much and believed the best for them. His doubts were gone and he decided to accept whatever happens.

He took a deep breath, looked up into the sky and nodded his head. With that he drove home to a pile of laundry, a dog wagging his tail, and much ado in the house. He smiled as he looked around thinking how blessed he was.

When Susan looked around her house at the mounds of laundry, she mumbled to herself that it was easier to pack than unpack. She took a cup of coffee and went out to the patio to enjoy the day. She remembered that on the way to the local airport, Nate had commented that he hoped they would all come back. Here they were all home. Actually she thought to herself that they were all better off as they learned so much about each other. She had a new appreciation for another culture that was a new experience for her. She heard the car in the driveway and was surprised that Brad had come back rather than stay at the work site. Nice!

Better yet, he brought a cup of coffee out to the patio and looked at his wife who was smiling at him. Together they sat listening to the yard sounds. They could hear Nate playing trucks in the sand box nearby.

Peter and Adam had decided to take Buddy to the creek to try to catch a few fish. They did not speak much. Buddy stretched out on the grass.

Adam said, "Even Buddy is happy to be home. He must have missed us."

Peter yawned. He was thinking of his 14th birthday and wondered what his parents would be getting him this year. He hoped it would not start a cycle of events like the rifle did last year. Soccer practice was scheduled to start next week. He fell asleep on the grass.

Adam smiled as he looked at his older brother asleep on the grassy slope and reached over to pet the dog, Buddy.

Abby sat in the window seat thinking of Allie. If she only knew that Allie was swimming in the university pool in Beijing wondering what Abby was doing. Abby thought back to how all this started when they signed up for a pen pal in China. She had a new appreciation for her family and her life after the scare in the airplane. She took out her notebook to make some sketches and notes about the adventures from the time they received the letter from Sadako, the huge airplane, the guy who acted like a friend but actually was a spy for the Chinese government, Sadako's family, then the big fire at the plant, the Grand Canal, and the journey home on the airplane that almost didn't make it.

Then she jumped up to remind her mom that they had to get the peacock pin fixed for Grandma. Susan thought we are now back to normal.